RHERO DAD

SUPERHERO DAD

TIMOTHY KNAPMAN

illustrated by JOE BERGER

THE BIG BOOK OF PANCAKES

Dads can be quite ordinary, but **mine's** not, and I'm **glad,** because, **you see,** he's secretly a . . .

You can hear his **Super Snoring**
from a thousand miles away . . .

. . . so I jump up on his
tummy shouting,

"Come on, Dad!
It's day!"

He makes these
Super Breakfasts,
though he's only
half awake.

(So sometimes I'll get
toast with **chocolate**,
jam, ice cream
and **cake!**)

His jokes are
Super Funny . . .

. . . and his laugh is **Super Long.**

HA HA HA HA HA HA HA HA HA HA HA!

He can pick up
our dog Jumbo
so he must be
Super Strong.

Whenever we play dinosaurs, he does a . . .

ROoOoOOOAR!

like this.
And afterwards he gives
me a Tyrannosaurus kiss.

When he **zooms**
me round and round,
I feel like
I can **fly.**

And when I'm on
his shoulders,
I am **taller**
than the **sky.**

He's very good
at woodwork, too
(you're MEANT to
bang your thumb).